MW00946458

www.mascotbooks.com

Luno! The One Who Rode to South America on One Wheel

©2017 Cary Gray. All Rights Reserved. No part of this publication may be reproduced, stored in a retrieval system or transmitted in any form by any means electronic, mechanical, or photocopying, recording or otherwise without the permission of the author.

For more information, please contact:
Mascot Books
560 Herndon Parkway #120
Herndon, VA 20170
info@mascotbooks.com

Library of Congress Control Number: 2017904087

CPSIA Code: PBANG0517A
ISBN-13: 978-1-68401-326-5

Printed in the United States

This book is dedicated to

Lucy Morgan Gray

The fulcrum around which the Gray family
now lovingly pivots.

The Sustainable Adventures of

LUNo!

THE ONE WHO RODE TO SOUTH AMERICA ON ONE WHEEL

Based on the real tales of
Written and Foot-illustrated by **Cary Gray**

Luno!
Where are
you going?

Why
are you wearing
your backpack
and tying your
jacket around
your waist?

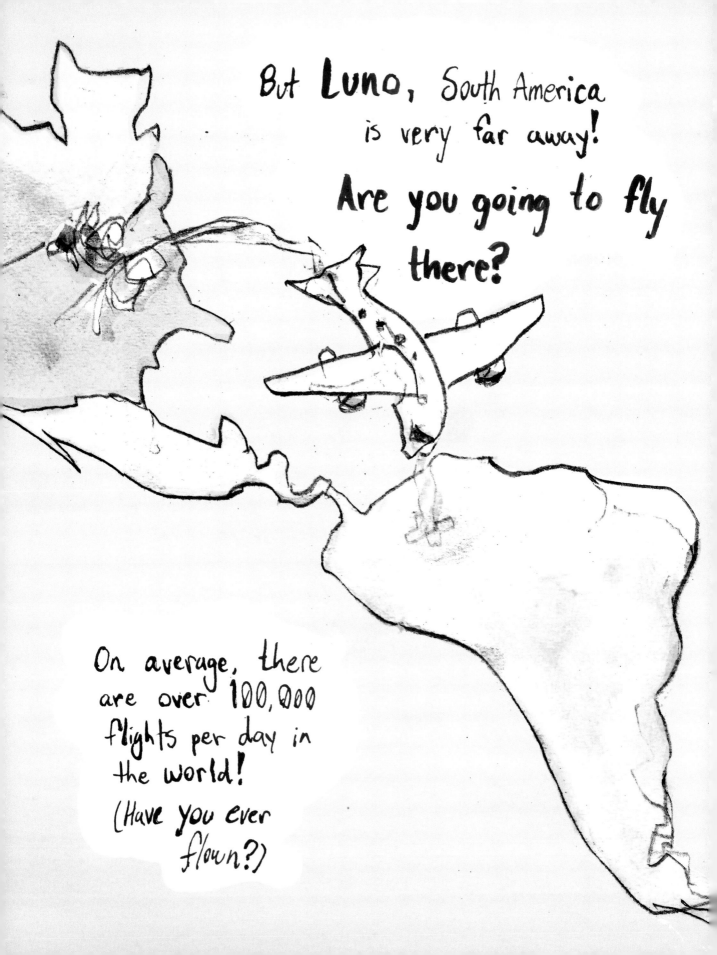

WILL YOU
go by bus or train, or will you
GO BY BEAR?

* If you see a bear in the wild, do not try to pet it or sit on its shoulders.
Stay away to be safe, and respect them.
Back away slowly, or if the bear approaches, curl into a ball and play dead.

But Luno, how?

Without a plane or a train, or a bus, or a bear, **how will you go that far?**

Anything is possible!

Except for talking llamas, of course!

Excuse me, young man, but I am an alpaca!

(* Alpacas are smaller versions of their cousins, llamas, which are used as pack animals in South America.)

I will stay away.

I can see and enjoy them from far away.

* We all share the world, but wild animals are not pets. Do not feed or approach them. Stay with a group when hiking where wild animals live. Do not leave food out.

I will leave no trace:

I will not leave food scraps or garbage.

We all take care of this world.

But **Luno!**
What about the rain?

Will you ride in the rain?

What about the snow?

Will you go through the snow?

What about rivers? Will you cross rivers?

Rivers are important sources of water for drinking and farming.

(Do you live near a river?)

Through rain and snow,
over hills and
through heat,
across rivers
I will go!

These make it an adventure. These are not reasons to give up! Follow your heart and follow your feet, be prepared, and you will make it!

I will see the St. Louis Arch on the mighty Mississippi River!

I was born here! Did you know that the Mississippi River is the longest river in North America, and third longest in the world?

(Do you know the world's longest?)

I will see the ancient temples of Mexico!

Many centuries ago, the Aztec and Mayan cultures built many large temples like this one, called "Chichen Itza." No, not Chicken Itchy — say "chee-chen eet-za!"

So Luno, when will you go on this adventure?

the END
... for now

Gratitude and Credits

Luno! was successfully funded on Kickstarter.com at 124% of its original goal. 101 lovely people gave $6,796. The story and spirit of *Luno!* belongs to you, and would not have been brought to life without you. Thank you:

    Chris Slydel, once again!
    Bridget and Susan Doughty, my former fellow summer swim teammates
    Colin O'Connor, my very good friend and co-conspirator
    Morgan and Lauren Gray, my brother and sister-in-law
    Jaime Sanders Giger, who first taught me ceramics
    Linda Kelley, scheduling assistant extraordinaire
    Erin Green and her blossoming family
    Buzz Weetman, fellow unicyclist
    Aunt Amy and Uncle Rick
    Aunt Meg and Uncle Denny
    Aunt Nikki and Uncle Mark
    Aunt Patti and Uncle Pat
    Stevie D, the "Bun" Man
    Debbie Murphy, unofficial aunt and fellow artist

Alicia Podmokly, Carl Hunt, Nuria, Diane Budde, Pong Lee, Darlene Crask, Susan Turner, Laura Danieri, Roxanne Pratt, James Bomgardner, Alex & Lauren Legrismith, TJ & Lilly Thomas, Jane Stevenson, Vitaliy Kulik, Ellen Miller, Alison C. Woods Baker, Juliana Bianes, Sasha Zemmel, Stephen Y, Frank Gladney, Deborah Aston.

Thank you to Tobey and Gordon for providing an awesome living/working space.

Thank you to Brandy and the South Whidbey Commons Coffeehouse for allowing me to work barefoot on this book, despite it being iffy, healthcode-wise.

The lovely folks at BR Printers in San Jose, CA
Kristie Cornelsen of Barrister's in Clayton, MO
Ed & Kay of the Whistle Stop Bike Shop in New Freedom, PA
Nichole Garrison of the Butterfly Garden Inn of Sedona, AZ
Tim and Monika Watson, for being awesome
Uncle Jamie and Auntie Gayle
Katlin Burley, for helping to edit and review
LoveJoy Finta, for his guidance, friendship, and mentorship. Thank you, brother.

Thank you to my two younger sisters, for being unique. I love you, you silly geese.
Thank you to my mom and dad for creating me, giving me my feet, hands, and encouraging me. (I'm diggin' Life.)

Thank you all.

About the Author

Cary Gray was born in St. Louis, MO in 1988. He was the second child of four and fully embodies the middle child spirit. Growing up, Cary built tree forts, rope swings over the small lake in his backyard, and in his teen years, large trebuchets (like catapults) capable of launching 9-lb rocks over 500 feet.

As an adult, Gray still spends much of his time in nature, where he prefers to be and to sleep. He has lived in a hammock 80 feet up in a redwood in California, and camped on a boulder in the middle of the Kootenai river. He spends his time writing, creating artwork, and giving talks to schools. He works to advocate for preserving natural spaces and biodiversity, as well as a healthy lifestyle.